Press the Bu̇tton of the Universe

by

Gabriel Saltan, 2023

ISBN: 9798379064464

Press The Button On The Universe by Gabriel Saltan

Press the button on the universe!

It may sound like a cliché but everyone has 24 hours in a day and everyone is given a body and an organ for thinking. These features of ours are "almost" identical.

However, it is significant if we can think at a higher level. If we can IMAGINE things at a higher level because that really makes a difference in the development of our lives. Here are some thoughts that you might be pick it up. Those thoughts like a tool to push and not just press the button on the universe but on your own universe to get what you really want from life!

If you have any then do so finally!

Let those who can understand it do so. Let those who can hear it what is to come to do so!

Introduction.

In one of my previous book, the core idea of the book came to me when I was at the lowest point in my life, perhaps at that point in my life emotionally lowest and in all other aspects as well. I clearly remember how I sat in a fast food restaurant middle of a very adventurous trip, in Brasov Romania in East Europe, and clutching a hot chocolate, I wrote the outline of my book on the paper napkin of the restaurant and summarized the thoughts and principles that defined my life and saved (me). I learned and concluded the lesson there and then, which I didn't always manage to apply, but at least I became aware of connections. That's when my book "Anonymous loser: Learnable skills for winning" was born.

https://www.amazon.es/loser-Learnable-skills-winning/dp/1521126046

Now I'm sitting in a completely different environment, I don't think I should run away from the cold or starvation or anything similar but yes, I still have a hot drink with me. Promise I don't use the napkin of the 5-star hotel. I don't think my life is in crisis in any way, but still! Nevertheless, the guiding thread of this book has finally been formulated. I've been writing it in my head for a long time, parts were ready, but somehow the inspiration without (which a good-hearted person cannot write a book) didn't come together. Although writing is just a matter of discipline like many other things only required focus.

It`s a vocation - the vocation of this book is to reveal the unknown to you. It is about the uncertain, malleable future and the ways of shaping it. At the end of the day, I am struggling with the fact and how and how profoundly we can shape it. I will answer also, is it possible to control OUR WORLD?

Completely, comprehensively! This is what I claim and prove. I will tell you my proofs embedded in the lines because we are able to do.

Honestly, I'm writing a bit driven by that inner tension, as a kind of excitement of a new experiment. In the meantime, I trust. I'm right, and I control my world, to the fullest extent. (I can feel your doubts in my brain about how you read it) The pain often stems from the inner uncertainty and tension that all of us want to believe we can control our lives. But more than once, many times the environment sends signals as if we have no say in everything that happens to us. Why does life take you where it takes you? This drift or drift is a word that lacks control and direction. And if we don't have control, then we may have to accept, or worse, put up with the fact that we are a kind of puppet in a program for the rest of our lives.

I wonder who could put up with that?

Of course, some can humbly and crawl before it. Kowtow and agree with it. So to say, this is what the machine threw at them like in Las Vegas or this is what was written for them. Just is it karma, which the belts are?

In my case, I am the one who cannot put up with being a cog in the machinery of the universe, a being without willpower and free control rights, an object without the right to dispose of being just an object on the world's gaming table. That`s why observed the inner game of life.

For years I have been collecting evidence and concluded I am absolutely right this. I am obsessed and sick of the compulsion force of life. I was born to control my life, and I am quite good at it! I have yet to find anyone who did or wanted better than me, or who cared for me even a little permanently. The world is made up of selfish individuals, and that's okay, you don't need to change it, life is wonderful because everyone can get what they want, and others are the same way, and they don't have to be winners and losers against each other.

If you too are influenced by the idea of being in full control of your life, then stick with me! By the way, the other side of this coin is depression.

Chapter I

A proof test, how I made a scientific experiment!

There are theories in life and there are practices that don't always overlap, and that's definitely a problem!

I have to tell you about a very improbable previous proof attempt of mine, from which we can learn a lot. The essence of it was that I was asking for something that I would be extremely unlikely to receive by chance anyway. However, let me walk you through the theory first, before I fully explain the specifics.

Well, perhaps we both know this much about physics, that the material world that is visible to us is not what it really is, but the sum of the things that our eyes can recognize, and the things that our brains create, that we perceive and become aware of. In other words, what our eyes cannot perceive is not visible to us.

But can it still exist!?

What our eyes perceive, but our brain cannot recognize, that is, form an image of, will not be visible to us in the same way.

But can it still exist!?

What our eyes perceive, and our brain is also able to create an image of by incorporating it into its system, but it does not enter our consciousness, because we do not pay attention to it, it does not even exist for us. In other words, if something does not rise above the threshold of our consciousness it does not exist for us.

But it still exists!? - (Stop here for a minute to take a break and think!) - Or does it not exist?! Maybe read the last

Press The Button On The Universe by Gabriel Saltan

few paragraphs again and conclude with your final belief.

Going further along this line, the whole world that we perceive as the material is actually a wave-energy – field only, that is vibration, that it does not material itself, but only consists of its countless possibilities. How it is assembled into matter, substance, and the perceived world is called to live and determined by the OBSERVING consciousness. The way you look for it is the way you get it. In the past, this was written in such a way that it is given as soon as you ask for it. But many people may not interpret that thought structure in this context.

The structure of the Universe, the Newtonian word, the Relativistic, the Quantum, and Quantum gravity as called: membrane or just "brain". I do not go further in the hyperspace and warped-brain I hope you are glad.

In the quantum field, nothing exists without observing consciousness or nothing materializing at the quantum-atomic level. (Now we will not go into whether there is an ultimate consciousness above us)

Let's think about an example in which a hundred people are lined up side by side in a dark room, crammed in, and each of them is holding a flashlight in their hand, pointing it at their face. If you call someone's name into the room, the person who hears their name will turn on the flashlight and illuminate their face, and this way you can find them and recognize them.

This is how consciousness works in the wave field, if you call out what you are looking for, it will appear for you, at least when examined at a simple quantum level, it works somehow like this. I have a few very good friends who working on physics, specialising in quantum physics and gravity waves. They confirm this example good enough for the general public.

Well, I know that this is completely unimportant to many because you only want to know and control your world that exists at the atomic level and above. Or I'll go even further, not even there, you just want a new apartment, a new car, a partner, or something more materially easier to grasp that will be a part of your life, and you see it as a necessity of your life. I can completely accept that. I am no different, and maybe we are normal because the influence of our environment does affect us. Why did I share this with you, do you think that as above as below, as small as large, the world was built based on a kind of logic? I think Einstein thought about this too. Even in ancient Egypt, they said such things or just read something from Indian Vedic books.

In other words, if you examine a glass of water or the size of a pool, does the structure of the water change? Not very much, right? Only the unit of measure and the order of magnitude. Here comes my conclusion, that what the observing consciousness "shouts" into the wave field on a small scale (on a quantum level), the wave field is collapsed by this spirit energy package by the observing mind, and I observe the quantum that I was looking for, so why can't the same work on a large scale? In my large real world? What law tells me that I cannot seek anything in the world that I can find, then I can get?

This search and observation take place in such a way that the conscious mind determines in theory what it assumes is there or should be there. What it assumes can be there. After that, it starts to spy on the horizon of the meter's instruments to see when the thing that needs to come appears because it will surely watch it. This is a very strong example if you can understand and apply it somehow.

I don't think there is any legality against this. As above, so below! What I didn't know at the time was actually what the subconscious was looking for. But if we knew that, we wouldn't call it subconscious, would we?

Guided by this train of thought, I started my experiments years earlier, first testing the theory with something that I thought was completely unlikely to happen by chance. In addition, like all scientific experiments, I tried to document this as scientifically as a layman can, and with notes data etc. Of course, I didn't dare to honestly admit to others what I was doing with it at the time. Maybe you don't despise me for it, since you too have seen the smiles of incomprehension on the faces of your friends and relatives. So I said the following: I'm asking the universe for a spoon, the kind with a four-leaf clover ending, the kind of little coffee-spoon that I can't find in an antique store because it would be very obvious that it's not produced by the universe, but I'll just go to a store to get it. So the point was that someone had to give me a teaspoon with a precisely described and even drawn shape. So finding it on the street doesn't matter, but someone who says it's yours! Gifted.

Receiving a car, apartment, gifts, or dinner invitation is likely, although not every day, but just one such thing, moreover, I thought receiving it is not very common, unusual, and certainly corresponds to my little scientific experiment.

So far, I don't know what kind of believe-it-or-don't-believe thought process has formed in you, but I will continue the process I started. I planned practical steps to get my spoon. I was so determined that I began to use everything I had learned before to attract my spoon. More precisely, every morning and evening I read that someone would give me such a small spoon! I asked the universe for it too! I may have even prayed, asking the Lord to give me such a small spoon. Of course, maybe I was a little overwhelmed with guilt at the time, that I was doing nothing less that I was trying to use God for what I was doing.

Maybe if I remember correctly, I worked on this for about 7 months, and persistently repeated my request to the universe, the spirit of the lamp, etc., just to finally get that frick... spoon. You can probably feel the strong

Press The Button On The Universe by Gabriel Saltan

emotional factor that developed in me at the end of the process. Of course, I didn't get anything. You won't change the universe, but if "IT" wants to sleep with you, and you're <u>ready</u> for it, and you're willing to do it, you'll have it.

Then, somewhere in the process, try to force the universe to give me what I demanded stopped. I was tired, tired of trying, I didn't believe in it so much anymore, and for reasons like this, the daily routine somehow stopped then I let go completely.

I have to pause with the story here, so we can analyze what happened a little, and you can also draw parallels with your own life so that you can clearly identify what the steps were, and what was missing from my process.

●I decided what I want.

●I wrote it down exactly, and I also put a deadline next to it.

- I also drew a drawing.
- I read regularly, disciplined repeating what I wanted.
- I honestly wanted to prove myself.
- I had it on a small card with me, and in all the cafes I went to, believe me, I expected it to be such a small spoon and to be given to me.
- imagined and visualized

Honestly, I have never met such a spoon in the cafe shops. Somehow, this <u>conscious focus</u> seems to have repelled that nasty spoon. It was quite unique, I admit. Many times I regretted defining what I wanted so precisely. Didn't you walk like that, wondering why you didn't ask the world for less? Have you thought ever that you don't need the "blo.. millions" just to let the world at least give you food or pay your rent?

Press The Button On The Universe by Gabriel Saltan

And lo and behold that crazy world refused to deliver the thing to me. You may have been in a similar situation, where you did your things by following most of the steps suggested by the self-development literature and you did everything possible (that is what you think you should do).

But if you haven't figured out what you're missing from these steps, I'm writing just for you!

Let's be fair, at the time I didn't even know what the missing steps were, but maybe I'm formulating a general law now by saying that.

If we want to get somewhere but we're not there after a while, and we're still not there a little while later neither, then SOMETHING is missing. Then we don't know SOMETHING yet. Yes, or yes?

So it is better to know that ignorance cannot be replaced by patience because it is equal to stupidity. I mean the ignorance of acceptance the fact, the existence of lack of understanding and lack of knowledge even if we know a lot.

First of all, I lacked the emotional deep vibrating feeling, the deep desire. To desire something with a white glow, like iron.

You can't just create something in the world, there's no such thing as conjuring something with your wand and something meaningless appearing out of nowhere.

It's just that an important image imbued with emotions strives to be realized immediately, and even appears immediately out of nowhere. Time is existing only because we agree on it as humanity.

You can't often create things for yourself out of nothing, because the things you think you want don't really mean anything to you.

I repeat once more that if you want to receive something, even if it is logically necessary for you and important to you, you will not receive it, and you cannot receive it, because it means nothing to you and you do not feel anything for it.

The world does not supply your logically, consistently necessary needs. The need is not an essential factor in the equation. But the emotion, the deep hot desire, even if it's stupidity. The throbbing unbridled emotional storm is the factor. I try to use good words what are describe and that reflect the emotional depth that creates this call. In other words, it creates and thus maintains continuous concentration.

So, even if your roof has a hole, you won't have extra money for roof replacement either, because it doesn't mean anything to you. It's bothering you certainly but still not emotionally good enough for creation. The life on Earth is put together in such a way as to emotionally force as many of us as possible into this state of not really meaning anything. However, there is no such thing as a system running without energy input, something must cause something. The cause-and-effect relationship is general and applies here as well.

In other words, if you need something, you'd better create a strong emotion for it, otherwise, you'll not have a shot at conjuring it into your life. Just think about the power and energy that is the result of you being here on earth with us. We may be the result of a flash of intense, powerful flash but we are undeniably so. My treasures this your parent`s action was.

And from here on, we have to talk about how you can rise above your emotions, that is your emotionless state of mind now. Maybe it's time, and as we grow older, the amount of our experience accumulates. We are less and less able to take illogical, stupid but passionate and at the same time, energetic steps and thanks to these passionate emotions start and accomplish things. Over time, more and more experience accumulates in us and our brains, which leads to logical analytical steps. What is actually the memory of our previous painful experiences, and our mind tries to protect our soul and our life from future suffering? In other words, the cold mind, the brilliant logic kills the energy of brutal strong desire and creative imagination, dreams, and the emotional attraction capable of creating. Do not mix and do not misunderstand this explanation, you still can be a billionaire based on logic. The frontal lobe part of our brain kills the power plant capable of creating. Knowledge and analysis are the enemy of creation, of desire, of blinded, often animal instinctual emotions. Strange isn't it?

This is why so many people rationally reach the point where they already know and want more and take the steps leading to it, but the whole thing is empty, the whole thing lacks the creative energy that creates the whole world. As well as constantly reproducing.

Think of the moment when you can practically create, think of when the delicate breath of orgasm or ejaculation leaves your lips! I know it's a strange change, but if you want to get close to this emotional state and want to identify what the creative moment is like that creates things, then you have to know it and learn to stimulate this creative thought, which does not mean, don't get me wrong, that you have to start a sabbatical lifestyle.

The thoughts of mine another approach to explain. Associated with this law, when you have a lot of goals and desires present in your mind but on the other hand, those goals are emotionally empty, at the moment when another kind strong emotion is filled with fear pop in your mind, - but the fear is also an emotion, especially is very strong one -, you will immediately receive something manifested full of fear, the trigger is a strong emotion.

If you repeat your money mantra or your relationship mantra, but it dawns on you that you might lose again, then if it is a strong emotional flash, you can immediately get the object of your fear. Analyzing and quantifying this subject a little. Up to 40-150 thoughts per minute, which is close to 100,000 a day while you are awake what we have! Even one, the <u>thousandth</u> is enough to be able to create. Even if it has a negative effect on you! This is both good and unpleasant news!

It kind of works like what happened to me recently in England. Due to a traffic situation, I had to call the general police number. A voice soon picked up, to whom I began to tell my situation before he interjected something like: is there a direct threat to life or injury? When I told him that we were here and had called them before, he interrupted again and repeated his question. To which I had to answer that there was obviously no danger to life or similar risk. The answer to that was to hang up the phone, c'mon! Do not use the line for anything other than what it is intended for.

This is how the universe works, it only PROVIDES resources for your affairs if the answer to the question is: what do you think is a vitally important, serious matter on your part? If the answer is a heartfelt YES. Then you get everything right away. Stop to think! Enjoy what you got!

Or another cute example, let's say you had angels who take care of taking your needs at the wish-fulfilling office. Their job is to try to deliver every wish and to have it fulfilled by the higher heavenly power. However, as in all offices, some officials assess your wish needs, and when your angel gets there, does he have to fill out the part of the form asking if the request is serious?

So are you serious? Degree of seriousness? The water not boiling on

99 Celsius, you cannot be 80% pregnant. Are you or not, fact check.

The regular answer is NO, he's not that serious. In such cases, the unnecessary, not really important things are just waste, and then there would be no room for true dreams, so they cannot be fulfilled, OBVIOUSLY.

That is, they reject it. Your angel can go home again with empty hands. So, if you don't want to push the angels, don't do it to the poor.

Back to hunting for my little spoonbill. I started doing things that gave me nothing but joy. I started travelling, wandering around. To fly here and there, just to see the world. I simply sped up my daily routine. My brain, which was pulsating every day, started to spin up with unusual, unknown things. I remember the first time I was able to see the Colosseum in this way. I only had 40 minutes to find it for the first time in my life in Rome, during a transfer and to at least see what the pile of stones was like and to reach the other train that I had to go on. The rush, and the way my nerves were burning, whether I would get lost, whether I would reach it? To this day, which train goes and how is vividly on my nerves. Ever since then, the most beautiful caress to my nerves is when I can sit in a pub (sorry, restaurant) next to the Colosseum and remember that day while sipping pleasant drinks. I made a deep memory in the Gladiator restaurant.

Then I began to crumble a sentence in my mind from the Bible. "Watch and pray!" I wondered a lot about what it might mean?

Because of that, even the sentence and what to say can be very powerful.

In parallel with all of this, I started training and playing sports again regularly and in a planned forced way like preparing for a race.

During the vigils, I learned a lot, read courses and classes, read 2-3 books per week, and inspired the nerves of my mind with new, different, unusual impulses. Adventures. This time borne the idea of Adventure of Gabriel Saltan.

I wrote down and set goals, without any rational, real starting point or any rational existence of basics. I have written about the fact that I travel abroad at least once a month and explore Europe. I was totally broke that time. I brace myself and set off with my son, and the two of us drive across the continent in a car, we go as long as we want, we stop we see things we want, and that's how we wander, father and son. Everything like that was absolutely impossible and irrational according to my reality at the time. It was just as likely as someone who doesn't even play the lottery, winning the lottery. In a word, I want to express that I tried to spin my brain to such an extreme speed that it was absolutely above normal by staying awake long nights, dreaming, reading, and doing sports. Kind a life how the shaolin monks started their practices. Lot of meditation, etc, and then required physical activity for a good health.

Perhaps I would also say that in my brain I felt almost better in my dreams - underlined, I felt in my dreams - than I did when I was awake.

Then, something happened that was the change. Changed, from one week to the next, where I live. My environment. Everything usual until then has changed, and it has taken over for a snap. It was just like a quantum leap at the subatomic level. Looking at the time plane of my life, I was suddenly present in two places at the same moment, exactly what you were paying attention to, I was present for you in that reality. If you had been an external observing consciousness at that time in my life you so that.

I call this "time-experience", this lawful experience, is "TIME BREAK". This is an experience in that you only realize what is going on when you are already in the new QUANTUM position when the desired change has already BEEN CONCLUSION and IMPLEMENTED.

Then my long-forgotten experiment resurfaced. One pleasant morning, a person very dear to me approached me with a cup of coffee, put it on a tray in my lap, and the words left her lips, which were about giving me a spoon as a gift (just like that) on a tray.

Bammm! The shocking atomic bomb in my brain.

Needless to say, I sat frozen for minutes, speechless, staring at the exact scoop I expected from the universe, the angels, or whoever. I asked and it was given, exactly as it was described as needed.

Honestly, when all this happened, and the realization exploded in my mind, I did not fully see this process, I did not recognize its laws that led to the realization. Even though I KNEW about all of them even then. In other words, in order for it to work for you, you don't necessarily have to understand it as deeply as I do. Moreover, if you wait in your life to understand it all, then you will never, NEVER actually understand it, mainly because you want to understand a world what is created by many of us. What is just created, which is only now being born by us. By the time you get to know and understand it, it has moved on and changed maybe.

I would emphasize that action usually leads to the desired state, whatever it is, the material world can be operated on material grounds for you. The problem with many creators, universalists, and gurus is that they want to manipulate the universe because they are TOO LAZY to go out for it. In other words, they want something in exchange for nothing, which is a dead idea. Just imagine how complicated for the angels to provide your wish, they have to break into your house, kick your door, if you are just sitting in your dark room, or front of your Pc. This game has to play outside.

The other chapters of the book will guide you in that what you can discover for yourself in this very powerful story, we will analyze and magnify the information, but in fact, you already know everything here between the lines.

In any case, it will be better if I draw your attention to it as a kind of warning in the user manual. It's not a silly thing for stupid people to say that hot chocolate is hot.

This is a warning that it is better to prepare, and that it may hurt, and it is very certain that when it comes to change or development, it may come with pain. The nature of pain is that unexpected pain hurts. If you can prepare to receive an injection, then it is not so painful, you know you have to relax, and it stings, it hurts a little.

But this kind of change is unexpected, these changes that await you on the road are unexpected QUANTUM leaps. I can only tell you one thing, where I was before, everything I wanted and dreamed of would have been impossible in that environment, and I got everything in one package, but it hurts like a newborn is hurting but required for a new life.

If we continue together despite these, I wish you a good adventure, and let's look deeper into the rabbit hole together, how looks a day when you going to try to apply!

Chapter II.

Is about expectations, goals, clear calm thoughts, and a clear mind on the way, listening the inner voice, and beliefs.

I like to play, and life without games is boring.

Let me bring to the table a life story with lessons, from my busy everyday life. Not something what you can see on YouTube where somebody shows a life what is not real and related with yours. Watching a tour around the Earth is not maybe your day by day reality (yet).

I got into a situation where I had to meet a tight deadline like you have some similarities surely. I had to get from one place to another with a very short deadline and to make it even more difficult, I had to solve the task without my vehicle. There was an opportunity for someone to offer their vehicle, but that would have been too easy to solve, so it didn't even come up. The favour that needs to be asked always waits for a return, it's better if the other half of the person keeps the balance of the favour positive. I don't owe it to someone else.

So the vehicle as a transportation chance was lost, and getting a ride from someone else was not an option either. That left me with the means of transport reserved for the masses, the public transport, and my extras are my legs.

The journey was from one place to home and after going to another place. Of course, I reserved the option of solving the situation with a taxi but in addition, to complicate my situation, I set a budget in case I have to solve the transportation in both directions by taxi. I immediately took all the money and cards out of my pocket, and there was left in only what I intended to pay for this purpose. You can say I'm totally crazy, but I can tell you to believe what you want. This is just an exciting game, don't spoil someone else's good game with your opinion!

OK, so I left one place a little late than planned, but I arrived home, took care of my hygiene needs, and was ready to go to my other location.

Have I looked at exactly how I will go? – <u>NO definitely didn`t.</u>

Of course, I looked up how to get there in the Map application, but I didn't specify my plan, it wasn't that. I had to leave my door at 19:45. The planer app told me that the journey will be 1 hour and 15 minutes but nothing more than that and nothing more precise. When it comes to serious things in life, you can say, I'm pure crazy. But what an exciting game it is! Some of my friends would say that is insane action I say is simply living a life with belief.

Back to the story: meantime, I responded to a momentary important message because it interrupted me. Then, when I slowly <u>felt</u> I have to leave now! I decided that now would be the time to leave, which I did. <u>So I acted.</u>

I got off, and at the first bus stop where my map helper suggested connecting, I was only 15 seconds late to reach it. Maybe the interruption was the reason, maybe the inner planer was designed this way?

I wasn't worried because I knew I would get there, I knew I would be there in time, I had no idea how I was going to do it, but I knew. With that calmness, I started to walk to the next point where I assumed the next bus connection will be waiting to pick me up.

Well, that's after a ten-minute walk, I happened to be on the opposite side of the road when the bus arrived and by the time I got through the driver grumpily indicated that he had already left. There was no chance of him picking me up.

At first, I wasn't worried because I thought another bus with the same sign would come soon. Which I thought was half right because not minutes but after 45 minutes, which would have caused a very, very significant delay.

Then I thought, or listening to some inner suggestion, I decided to choose the other direction, which is apparently evasive! I was confident that even if it was a detour on that road, I would still get there sooner than if I wandered here. There was a moment when I almost started waiting for the next bus, which was going in the same direction, but since it would have taken me to a completely unknown area, I decided not to wait. Something inner voice told me NOT TO STOP, to KEEP MOVING, to MOVE TOWARDS THE GOAL, be MOVED, and act.

Let's note here that the main rule is: NEVER WAIT! If you want something, go and reach for it, go out for it, go in front of it, but definitively don't wait.

I did so, that is walking again towards the stops on the other street. Which I did in a few minutes. The first bus arrived and I wasn't sure if it is the right bus, but since it just arrived I asked the driver if it was going in the direction of my goal. The answer was yes. So I immediately decided if it takes ME CLOSER TO MY GOAL then I will take it and move towards with it, if not perfectly right there but CLOSER to the goal, in the direction. I didn't wait for the situation to be perfect.

On the bus, I would have started to find out on my phone how the timetables were then, and exactly when and HOW I WOULD do. WHAT and WHEN TO TRANSFER, BUT thanks to the exceptional situation in the morning, (of course, I was in a place with my phone where, due to the lack of coverage, the phone it was looking for the network all day) the phone just died and it said goodbye to me. I stacked back in the last century, no technology just guardian angels and beliefs. Required different abilities.

So there won't be a route guide either way.

But don't worry, I wasn't worried at all, I told myself that everything would be fine. As long as I remember the road, I will go. From there I`ll get lost or hail a taxi on the road because it already fits into my budget and since I had no more cash in my pocket, this situation was given and fixed. Sounds insane, isn`t it?

So I travelled with confidence for the next 20 minutes and got off at the right stop. Yes, but the next stop is a walk again, it's only 400 meters, but a walk. When my connection passed me at the 300th meter. I was very happy to be able to make sure that there are buses that go even here, next is only one hour later.

But don't worry, since I'm already closer and there was no reason to worry, I'll hail a taxi while I walk closer to the supposed location.

I didn't stop to wait. I went, on the stop lane with my back to the direction of travel, then 1.5 kilometres long, when the first taxi appeared. I waved, I waved, and I even jumped a little. I stopped it successfully. Yes, but it turns out that he won't take me because he came for another order, and I'm not called Miss Gloster, and he can only take her.

Never mind, colleague, say on the radio that another car is needed here! The Pakistani driver answered that way he just simply handed me a business card with the number of the taxi centre on it. Says to call them. Bye.

You can imagine how much I was laughing inside, and I had no desire to explain this whole process to the driver. But don't worry, I can be almost there, that is closer now. But by now I've lost track of time. I knew it wasn't too late, but I had no idea how long it would be, and of course where exactly my location was. I knew the address, but I didn't know where it was.

The main thing is to keep walking because something scared me that somewhere on the map, I had to cross where I guessed the way. Which in reality, let's be honest, was a very nebulous and confusing idea. But I knew I would get there somehow in time. There was tension in me but MY MIND was cold and could remain optimistic despite the tension. Then in one of the roundabouts, as I passed through, I had already gone about 300 meters. Suddenly I changed my mind. I wondered if I should continue my journey on the other road. Until finally, I had the FEELING, MY INNER SUGGESTION, that I must turn around and go on. If it doesn't lead me directly to where I need to go but a bit beside it, a bit detoured but it will be, it might be the best route for some reason. Strange.

Then I started to rationalize this, that there are more taxis there, or that another bus will go there, etc. Actually, I dared to follow an inexplicable inner suggestion. Which of course is not inexplicable, because I'm explaining it right now. As I observed a taxi that left the roundabout just one exit earlier. It could not have seen me, I wasn't even surprised anymore, I just kept going, like a dog after a smell, just kept going. I went, following the direction dictated by the suggestion.

Then, as soon as I went around the corner, it dawned on me that my favourite gyros, which are open from five to midnight, must be right around the corner. Earlier, I thought about the hotel next to them, that I would call a taxi with the receptionist there. But it would have taken too long to get to the hotel, so I rejected it in the first place, due to the loss of time, because I had a deadline.

It would have been more certain from a rational point of view, but not by the control, relying on the control!!!!!!!!!!!!!!!

Well, I went to the Kurdish guys and told them that they should do me a big favour as a regular customer, and now! I need a phone to see how close the location is. What he did for me, only 3 kilometers. The next thing is that I should be thrown there, quickly saving my situation. What I emphasize is that it was not lost for a moment, even if to everyone else who examines it, it may have seemed very under-planned and under-organized. But for me, who learned to live with expectations and to let myself be CONTROLLED by my suggestions, it was not under-planned, because someone, something else very, very seriously, as you can recognize from what has been written, organized it for me. I just had to go forward in the direction of FAITH. Perhaps I don't need to say that at 20:59 my gyros guy, my delivery driver stopped at the address. I offered money to him, which I had intended for a taxi, but he didn't accept it. I wasn't even surprised, everything happened according to plan. In other words, my plan was only to be there exactly when I needed to be. I had an inner certainty that I will be there at the right time. I HAD NO DOUBTS ABOUT IT THE ENTIRE WAY.

Well, whoever has ears, whoever has the sense to hear, and understands the message inherent in what has been said. Here is the map for anything, anywhere you want. Practice and practice, that is just playing and playing, because the game is GOOD!

Chapter III.

Thoughts on how masters appear in our lives and how we can use these opportunities? Also, a few fruits of wisdom may taste are likeable to your mind.

Somehow, people, their sentences, and uplifts appear strangely! They appeared at your beck and call, or they are part of the ramifications of your life.

Every time you enter that stage in your life, the right person, phrase, or upliftment appears out of nowhere. You have to live by faith and EXPECT that it will appear. A searching mind finds them, but that's it!

The probing mind that searches for answers and solutions will find them as soon as it knows exactly what it is looking for. If you see it and know it, it will appear.

If you can't find it you're not looking, or you're not looking very well.

Not every upliftment-step on your way up can stay with you, but they were necessary to get up, so don't be angry with your servants-stairs when they leave you, they're just giving up their place, they're just needed somewhere else, they can't always be with you, someone else needs them too.

I recommend that you never try to step into the same river again, and there is never a way back that will take you forward to a new goal. If you left something behind, it was for a reason. Changes are good, it keeps your mind and soul fresh and sharp. It is not particularly wise to go back somewhere to start again what you have already put aside for some reason. Of course, you may need to finish your roof before the monsoon rain comes.

Related to others and the loneliness. Be aware if you move away totally from people with your activities on this planet, you may move away from the planet from life too. Also, give back to the universe, because you get to feed on it, and serve people and you will find enough people who deserve it. If I serve enough, my environment will be filled with such people after a while and there will be no room for other attitudes around me. I didn't learn this right away the first time. It takes time to gain wisdom.

For greater things, you need greater masters.

There are things that you get again as a tempting obstacle. Everyone will have expectations and opinions about you until you don't know exactly who you are, their opinion will matter to you. Maybe, on the other hand, if life puts a lesson in front of you, again and again,

Press The Button On The Universe by Gabriel Saltan

then maybe you get it because you should finally learn it. Ask yourself regularly what this situation teaches me or what should I learn about myself from this conflict. How should I change myself to benefit from this challenge?

If you live long enough and your soul stays fresh for long enough, you might notice that life can repeat itself. It's even lucky that you didn't have to die to have another chance to do something that pops up again.

Building a life is a step-by-step process, you have to build it up, just like you build a house. You put the bricks one after the other, sometimes you build walls, and sometimes you go for bricks because you can't be in two places at the same time. Sorry, then SOMEONE realized that quantum and quark exist, and something can be in two places at the same time. So now they've messed you up pretty well with this one, so you might as well be successful in one fell swoop.

(successful equal, you achieved what you wanted in your own terms.)

I RATHER DECIDED THAT I WANT THE SOLUTION RIGHT NOW, IT IS ALREADY HERE IN MY LIFE, AND I HOLD IT IN MY HANDS. And you can live according to your faith if it makes you happier. As you think, if it's good for you...? Do you compromise, back down, and no longer dare?

Do you know, the excess will spoil anyway why have money that you don't have a place for? What you can measure can be developed, and what you observe will develop. Wealth, like a woman, if it's not important to you, she senses it and won't stay with you.

At different stages of your life, you will receive different masters, and for different reasons, you will look at them with respect and consider them your master. There will be masters of chapters, there will be masters of the occasion, the master of the day, and thus masters of sections.

As soon as you get to know the master, you recognize his imperfection, which is useful if you accept it. You are not HIS JUDGE, you are his student. Don't trade the right thing with the wrong approach.

The conception of our divinity cannot set a limit to handling our weaknesses correctly and with the appropriate humility. Admitting our ignorance and inabilities, moving forward guided by the angels.

Sometimes, with your master, you think that you are better than him. You know more than that. I don't need him

Press The Button On The Universe by Gabriel Saltan

because you know better. You may be right about these, but the master and the prentices are not together because the student can recognize his master's mistakes, but so that the prentice can answer the question properly. Am I successful, am I an achiever? And discipleship can legitimately be sustained as long as the disciple is not better and the prentice is a higher-level achiever! So that's why they're together! In other words, as long as you don't make more and better shoes, faster, it's back to the gallows. You got your master for a thousand reasons, stay with him until then.

In waters that are new on the sea, in heights where you have not been before, you need new and local people who can lead. Understanding what they say is not the same as doing it, or knowing the same thing.

Just because you get older doesn't mean that just because you've heard those things more than once, you understand them better or that you can act better. It means many times, it has happened several times over the years, that you haven't heard or learned something again. So instead of being arrogant, just pay attention, what are you still not doing? Be a little honestly critical of yourself, just enough so that your self-esteem and faith in yourself don't collapse.

So think about the masters in your life like this, and one day you will become one. I pray for that by then you will be prepared for the burden of responsibility that people will pay attention to you also do not forget you as a master can learn from a prentice you also got that prentice for a reason. Take off your high horse and observe and learn and adopt.

Chapter IV

Is about having to choose because you can't have everything at once.

I know how tempting to have everything on earth with this knowledge and how to press the button of the universe, but as I know well you are not quantum, we are just materialized, humans. When you're young, without experience, and real, valuable, relevant knowledge, you don't get ahead easily. Then the lack of knowledge and previous gathering of experience sets the limit in progress.

But what happens when you are no longer young? There are times when someone can get there to gain the so-called life experience. When a face-to-face situation or a face-to-face person does not mean a new experience, but only a new repetition of the previous experience. What happens when what comes up, you can say that I've seen this a few times, I've seen how it will end a few times, so I know what kind of experience can be expected from this in the best and worst case. What happens when these situations no longer mean excitement or another adventure?

Then life can get boring.

But now let's delve into what happens if you are in a stagnant situation in your life and for some reason you don't know what to do next. For which you do not need to have a lot of experience, in most cases - pay close attention - it is sufficient that there are no external compelling circumstances.

Many of us are full of ourselves and our wonderfulness, even if there is little reason for this. Which, after all when we examine it, is a well-developed, wonderful tool of our soul's self-defence mechanism. Without it, we would wallow in the hell of deep discouragement and depression, sliding to the point of suicide, so it's not a big deal after all.

But the essential element of the point is that if no external circumstances are forcing us, we have little reason to tease ourselves that we should move because something has to drive us. Because why should you drive if you don't have to because only the "big" man has to! So, in the absence of this, we fall into a state called the comfort zone, which keeps us motionless and in soft warmth.

However, a question will arise (when life starts to put pressure on you), which is about what should I do, what should I do? Unfortunately, very few of us can decide this correct actions at that time of pressure. When there is pressure on us, it is not really us who decides, but the compulsion squeezes us into the closest situation we are close to.

Let me give you a visual description of this life stage. Think of it like when you walk up to the launch of a Mars tourist spaceship. In which seat you want to travel during the launch? Well, you sit here and there, for so long trying to decide which seat would be the best for you, that time passes and hip-hop kicks in. Then 6-7+ G acceleration will very easily squeeze you into the "nearest" seat, if not send you down to the floor, and then brother, you will travel there until the weightlessness stage surely.

I guess you have experienced such a situation before. You know exactly that was not your choice in your life but of course we tell everyone that this is what we wanted for ourselves, and how good it was to travel in that seat. That's why I'm telling you that. These are not choices, these are compulsions, these are not your life, these are just the leftovers from the main table. You are forced to live on scraps, and you beg for the crumbs that fall from the lunch table of life because you could not choose properly in advance, and I do not talk about your wealth, or toys even if some of you would measure the life in those currencies.

Let's go back to the main point, which is that you have to choose. We have two extremes, one is that we know too little and see not much of life as a youngster, or we have already seen too much of life and gained more than enough experiences. Whichever one you are closer to now?

Be aware there is a third element of the matter, YOURSELF without the right choice, it almost doesn't matter where you belong. Because those who don't even know what their options are, their real options in life are not given to them to choose from, because they don't know what they can choose from. Or when you already know a lot, it's also difficult because you can feel you experienced already and everything seems just a repetition.

I would like to explain this: You know that almost any monkey can get into a reality show, and you can be a star for 5 minutes, and you can also get on TV for a bit. Or you can register and have your own YouTube channel, and then you are a star on your TV. Or you could go to university, or you could have a degree in library or HR, which may not be good for a living, but at least you can say that you have a qualification, because it might make you stand out from the average. Or you'll have a business degree because that's just something more serious, right? Either you will have a degree in economics or a lawyer just because. But you could be a vagabond, you could go abroad to wash dishes, because it is said to be respected there, and there you should not listen to the family news of the ruler of the country, what businesses they run, how much money they have or stolen, and why you, the average person, don't belong among them. Maybe you should listen there too, but you wouldn't understand there in the beginning, until you realize that the problem is, you're not the KING there either. But you can choose to be a mayor or a board member, or you can be many, many other things.

Which one should you choose? I'm going to go further, you may be even more confused and in trouble about what you can choose from, because let's say become a railway worker. Yes, but I've already been. Then you should be a driver, but yes, I was already one. Well, then become a politician, and work for him, but yes, I was already one. You weren't a chef yet, but I was. Then let's say you become a writer, that presupposes such a free life, yes, but you had that too, then you become a lawyer, that .... ah don't continue, it seems you've already been that too. Then become a manager, and work with people, yes, yes, but I was already one. Do you work in a hospital... have you ever had one at a shopping mall? have you ever had one at an airport? Well, let's say you become a baker than a porter! I was already late.

Athlete? I had it! Teacher? Done! I was already one. Then, after all, what the heck with a sad nest you haven't been to yet, what could you be?? And it's a confusing situation to be in when you don't know what you're moving toward because you don't see what else interests you at all.

You know that it's not worth getting into anything anyway...... Or I already was, so why should repeat?

The same problem as an actor who has been in the field for a long time is what the next CHARACTER will be, what will be the next role, and by taking on it, he will find excitement in acting again. The only difference is that it's about your own life.

I have an offer for a role that you would be interested in, how about playing it yourself? But who you are? Just stop and think a few minutes to answer to yourself this question. Now only you and your book, take the time to clarify who you are? What rolls you have?

Beneficial to write it down.

-

keep writing I give you one clear page:

Now, the new character?

1. Please shape the character and choose characters and traits that suit you.

2. Then play yourself, or more precisely, please learn to play yourself. In the meantime, just think, have you ever been yourself? When you chose every role element?

3, You will also be the dramaturg!

Unfortunately, until you do this, you are not on the stage of your life just watching others.

It means that if you don't learn to choose from among the many options, you'll stay outside in the corridor, waiting for the casting couch. But the most difficult thing here is that you cannot be Romeo and Juliet at the same time, you have to choose as I said in the beginning. You have to choose in life too, and in return, you have to give up all the other roles that are offered to

Press The Button On The Universe by Gabriel Saltan

you, and you have to decide not to play them now.

You have to be able to let all others roll to go!

Do you now understand why you have to choose!?

Perhaps your biggest obstacle in the choice is a lot of knowledge, a lot of knowledge. A lot of indiscriminate information can therefore be toxic in setting a new goal and in realizing a new thing. From the point of view of your future, where is the healthy limit?

The danger is a lot of indiscriminate information. What does this mean to you? There may be too much news. Too much Facebook. Too much politics, and too many rumours about rich and poor relatives. There are too many problems at your workplace that you even notice. Too much attention on things that only occupy your time.

In your life, the moment you have chosen the roles and character elements, time will immediately play a big role. A drastic change takes place immediately. There is no time for everything at once.

The need of the psyche is to pass the time. Few of us can just sit quietly and do nothing, really nothing, just nothing. Our brain is not a stable, static organ that stops and starts, rather it speeds up and slows down, but it goes on. Just like the heartbeat, it doesn't stop, it just rests between beats. Thus, the brain needs constant stimuli, cyclical stimuli that keep our nerves above the stimulus threshold and allow the brain's electrical impulses to flow. A person will do anything to maintain this unconsciously of course. He watches TV, plays, hums, MORALIZE, talks with his fellow humans, etc. LET'S JUST KILL THE

TIME. If there is no external stimulus, the autopilot works. In fact, we spend two out of every five seconds unconscious.

But when you finally have a decision, a choice, time is immediately subordinated to what is needed to fulfil the chosen role. That will fill your time. You won't have a single minute that can be wasted on any other pastime.

Finally, let's talk about one more thing that may arise in your mind: do you have to choose?

Because you may even discover the meaninglessness of achieving anything in life, because time, like your sandcastle on the beach, will wash away whatever you build, and then why? You can't build anything for eternity.

Maybe think about why people build sandcastles. Mostly for the pleasure of the smaller members of the family, for their own fun, for the joy of creation, for the pleasure of the temporary enjoyment of beauty and the realized state, such things that form momentary happiness, a memory on the speeding axis of time. Perhaps the point is that there is a shovel, there is sand, there is a beach, and if this is already a given, why not build something for yourself and others, your loved ones, to see the smiles on their faces?

So I suggest you choose! I recommend that YOU choose! And build/create something that brings smiles to people's faces. Then when you're done with it, find another sandcastle.

Chapter V.

The hero of time, whom you don't even know about, - do you understand what he is doing here?

We look at our hero (who could also be the Spring Dragon) at the moment when he is surrounded by many enemies. In fact, we got a shot of 8 or even 10 evil-eyed, murderous-looking figures holding their machetes high, ready to swing, standing only a step away from him. In other words, they surround him and threaten his life! All of them, are ready to immediately take the life of our hero. Looking at this picture it is obvious, we can see that our hero is lost and in the next moment, one of his attackers will surely beat him to death. Despite the fantastic abilities well known in the movies, even if our hero were to avoid the first couple of attackers, there would still be plenty of others. It is impossible to escape! They are not novice attackers and since they will strike AT ONCE, we can see our hero lost, doom, and death just a blink of an eye away.

You can be our hero yourself, as your fierce enemies surround you. You are surrounded by your creditors, the anxiety of losing your job, the situation of no money, or lot of money and do not knowing who wants just use you, the lack of fate, and the LACK OF LOVE. Surrounded by your shattered days and broken health of mind or body. You are suffering, writhing in the prison of the shackles of your PRIOR promises. You must have experienced that state when your brain shuts down dully and doesn't switch back on for days or weeks so that you can finally think a little! Time just passes on the treadmill, and Easter or Christmas or New Year's Eve comes when you switch back and are horrified at where your life has been or where it hasn't moved an inch. When you switch back and start thinking, at that moment all the devils seem to want to attack you at the same time and they <u>DO</u>! The swipes are coming and YES they will kill you one way or another you are doomed!

Then the camera zooms in on our hero, who could even be you! We see that the film has suddenly slowed down. More precisely, our hero deploys his secret magical ability, which results in his perception of time speeding up compared to his surroundings and being <u>able to act in a different time dimension</u>. We see how, for our hero, he skillfully dodges the blows, which are approaching much more slowly now, and slips out of the ring of attackers surrounding him. At the end of the scene, the freed hero laughs and waves to his fierce enemies from afar, and they are forced to accept that they cannot destroy this hero, because thanks to his miraculous ability, this is impossible for them, since our hero RULES the speed of TIME!

Is it true that time passes more slowly for those travelling at the speed of light?

Is it true that if you are progressing faster in the void, your time passes more slowly compared to ours?

This hero could even be you!! Let those who can understand do so, let those who can hear do so and let's move on!

Chapter VI

On influence and influence in brief.

Someone, a wise person, said that if you are proud of the fact that you have achieved everything in life solely on your own, then you obviously did not try to achieve something great. Yes, it is possible to achieve things alone, but when it comes to significant big, really big things, the ability to involve others is decisive. There are roughly two ways to involve others. One is the path of money and power, that is you buy the workforce but you have to pay a lot and waste your money on salaries without a vision. The other way is to have a compelling vision, a really attractive meaningful vision that you use to encourage people to join you in making it happen. Also called a mission. Very few people have a mission, and especially a sense of mission. In the absence of this, however, the most essential element of a commitment is missing, namely, why do we do it all? What does it mean to us?

If the only point of your activity is that you get money in return, it is a waste of life and time. It just drains you, drains you and drives you to death. You can't expect people to support you in making money only. If there is nothing else you can offer them, then by all means think a little more, please.

Be aware that you definitely influence people. With who you are, what you do or don't do is an example or a counterexample of your environment. Either you influence them towards you or away from you, but you cannot avoid influence.

Personally, I believe that bringing out your best possible self is the best thing I can influence you to do. This change may not necessarily be pleasant, but just as the muscle hurts when it is being built, I take on the pain of the construction. Strong people are always grateful for a heavyweight treat and dead people don't have opinions, do they?

You can't influence, (that is help) those with whom you're not in a relationship, you're not in a bond with, or you can't influence them very much or at all. Therefore, the first step in this process is connecting and building a relationship. If people don't feel that you care about them, if they don't feel it, if they aren't certain in the realization, even surprising for them, that you listen to them and care about them, then they won't let you and you can't help them. I'll go on, if you ever fail and prove to them once that you don't care about them anymore, you'll lose your influence and even the whole thing will turn against you.

However, the influencer's role never remains empty. Someone always becomes influential in people's lives. Think about what people were made to do in Napoleon's time, then the king came back. Just think about Germany in the 1930s, and then they built Bolshevik socialism. Or let's think that Churchill's dream was a united, peaceful Europe, and now the British are leaving because something else has taken over the influencing role over their minds, and supporting with arms to kill more brotherhood Europeans.

People themselves rarely know exactly what they want, and especially if an influencer meets them, then even if they knew before, they rarely stick to what they thought up before. People strongly believe that they cannot be influenced, and this greatly helps people and interest groups to influence people without being noticed.

If you do this, always do it conscientiously, as it serves them, and their goals, so that they are happier and stronger because of you. Treat people consciously and responsibly, even if you need them.

After all, why not say that I think we should do this instead, it will be good for you! There is no harm in doing this, in fact, it serves, so why not do it? So we did it.

Chapter VII.

The Focus needs because we are in a two-second unconscious stage every 5 seconds on average.

I need this, this is what it looks like!

Where is one of these? Has anyone seen this? Where can I find it?

This is exactly what I need, this piece was missing from my board until now, and I was looking for this, and it fits right here.

This is what I wanted, this is what it looks like! Where was it, it's good that I found it.

Chapter VIII.

The Happiness chapter.

Happiness is a stage of being on the road. Happiness doesn't just happen by chance, you have to work for it. Moreover, it is the responsibility of the wisest and smartest person in your environment to ensure the possibility of obtaining happiness for others as well.

As your child grows, the basis of your happiness is your common goal to grow, become stronger, raise his head, turn around, stand up, walk, run, ride a bike, say a poem, then write a poem, and later teach a poem, then stand on his own two feet, but I hope your ultimate goal is that your child, as well as yourself, can be happy as an adult.

Yes, but happiness is neither theirs nor yours. It is not static, nor an object, but rather arises from movement, it is about the happy state of being on the road. When you are on track and moving towards your goals, that is your only happiness.

So how can you share a mission, a dream with your family, friends and children so that happiness can bind you together? Because great art is always being able to work on your children's happiness. For that, you have to be on the road TOGETHER!

Be a REAL person who can do this with adults too. I trust you, you can lead them not only in the first 12-14 years, but I also trust you that they won't only see you a couple of times a year, I trust you, they won't be locked in offices in their lives, because I trust you, you can figure out how to take out them to do something. So don't die without taking them far. Take them, because it's your beautiful burden to be happy ON YOUR WAY together.

Go on an adventure, adventure is on now!

Just a little warning at the end!

As you travel along the highway of your life each of you is in a different stage and you will perceive exactly from the book where you are stationed now. It is unlikely that all of you will understand even some of you will be opposed to some of the things that is posted here. May I emphasize each of you will be right in your right way because what you think is right, in your own state, isn't? This doesn't mean I'm judging you, and you shouldn't answer or comply with anyone or anything in any way. However, my ultimate freedom is yours as well and we don't have to conform to others either. The fact, the earth is still spacious and large enough for everyone, thanks to the creator, dreams of unlimited size can fit on earth side by side in peace.

The book has two parts as you read, the first contains two powerful stories and the second part content more philosophical, bullet points that follow from towards to the point where we may disagree in our views in the following, it could be the point that is one of the main roadblocks in your current life situation.

Just think about it, maybe you do not want to know and see things differently?!

Well, you're not right, but let's not rule out that I'm wrong especially because, dreams and goals are mostly not achievable in the same state of mind in which they were born. However, problems are excellent opportunities to solve them in an altered state of consciousness! Some call it progress!

Also, most of us learned our stereotypes and paradigms, that's why let me raise a question what is a final question. Whose lie will you live in,

Press The Button On The Universe by Gabriel Saltan

your own or someone else's, this is the essential question, and you will have a final own answer which will determine and decide everything in your life. But you have to choose, and you will.

Gabriel Saltan

Gibraltar, February 2023.

Printed in Great Britain
by Amazon

20072105R00052